Echoes of Eden

Glam Limo

Printed in the United States of America
ISBN: Softcover   978-1-969213-28-1
Published by: TwinVerse Prime
Publication Date: 10/13/2025

To order copies of this book, contact:
TwinVerse Prime
Phone: (725) 257-6538
clients@twinverseprime.com
www.twinverseprime.com/

TABLE OF CONTENTS

PROLOGUE

The First Light

In the beginning there was only the Eternal, whose presence was too vast for creation to bear. His voice became the shaping power, for His hands could not touch without consuming. At His word the heavens stretched wide, stars ignited, and worlds found their place.

From the heart of His design He formed Eden, a garden unlike any other place on earth. It was the source, the fountain from which life flowed into all creation. At its center stood two Trees. The Tree of Life carried the current that sustained breath and growth, flowing through rivers and roots into every living thing. Beside it stood the Tree of Knowledge, heavy with fruit that bore the weight of judgment and awareness, a power too great for mortal flesh. Together the Trees were not meant for eating, but for balance, conduits through which the Eternal's order pulsed into the world.

The angelic forces rejoiced as the world unfolded. They were born of stardust, radiant and full of knowledge, but unstable in innocence, unpredictable in their desires. Among them rose Morning Star, brightest of all, the highest in rank, radiant in beauty, the most glorious creation of the Eternal. Yet he was not chosen to walk in Eden.

For the Eternal knew that the garden required a different hand, one fashioned from the earth itself. And so, He formed Adam from the soil, breathing life into his clay. Adam bore no brilliance of starlight, but in his simplicity and innocence he was purer than the angels. To him was given a purpose greater than Morning Star's. He was to nurture Eden, to guard the source of life that fed the world.

This was the beginning of harmony. Yet within the heart of the brightest archangel, jealousy stirred. And the echoes of that envy would reach far beyond Eden, rippling through Cain's city, through the rebellion of the Watchers, through the rise and fall of nations.

The story of creation was only the beginning. The story of corruption was about to unfold.

CHAPTER ONE

The Shaping Voice

Before the first dawn, there was only the Eternal. His presence filled all things, yet no thing could contain Him. His glory was fire beyond fire, and no creation could endure His touch. So, He spoke, and His word became the shaping force.

"Let there be light."

And light was born. It poured through the void, racing across the heavens, seeding the birth of stars. Galaxies whirled at His command, suns blazed into being, and worlds awakened in their orbits. Where His word moved, matter obeyed.

The angelic forces were called forth from the first light, countless as sparks from a flame. They were made of stardust, radiant, strong, and filled with awareness. Each was given a role, a charge, a place in the order of creation. Their voices rose in songs that shook the heavens.

Among them was Morning Star. He was the highest in rank, most glorious in form, clothed in brilliance like no other. His presence gleamed with hues of gold and fire, his countenance brighter than the stars. When he lifted his voice in praise, the heavens rang like living thunder. To him was given honor above all, for he was the beauty of the host, the brightest reflection of the Eternal's splendor.

He stood at the side of the Eternal when the seas were poured out, when the mountains rose, when the skies stretched wide. He watched as rivers were carved, as forests clothed the hills, as beasts stirred from the dust. And when Eden was spoken into being, Morning Star beheld it with awe.

For Eden was unlike the rest of the earth. Its rivers gleamed with living waters, its air shone with purity, its ground pulsed with power. At its heart rose two Trees, tall and unshaken. One carried the current of life, feeding breath and growth into all things. The other held the knowledge of judgment and consequence, a fire meant only for the Eternal to wield. Through them flowed the energy that bound creation together.

The angelic forces marveled, yet none dared step too close. For Eden's heart was not theirs to tend.

Morning Star gazed long upon the garden, and though his voice still rang in praise, a question flickered like a shadow within him. Why was such beauty made, yet not entrusted to him? Why did the Eternal withhold the fruit that pulsed with knowledge, when he, brightest of the host, was strong enough to bear it?

The song of creation still filled the heavens, but for the first time, Morning Star's voice faltered.

CHAPTER TWO

The Keeper of Eden

The Eternal spoke, and the dust of the ground gathered. Clay drew together, shaped not by hands but by the command of His voice. A figure lay upon the earth, silent and still, waiting for the spark of life.

Then the Eternal breathed. His breath was not the fire that makes stars blaze or the thunder that shakes the mountains. It was a gentler current, the rhythm that moves through all living things. It filled the form of clay, and the still figure stirred.

Adam opened his eyes.

Light filtered through the leaves above him. Eden stretched around him in colors his eyes had never seen before. Rivers sparkled like silver threads. Flowers burned with hues that seemed alive with their own song. Birds swept across the sky, and beasts moved with strength through the fields. The air itself pulsed with life, fed by the roots of the two great Trees that rose in the heart of the garden.

Adam rose to his feet, unsteady but strong. His breath caught in awe as he turned to the rivers, the trees, the creatures. Each thing seemed to recognize him, as if it had waited for his hand.

The Eternal's voice came like waters flowing deep. "You are Adam. To you I give this charge: nurture My garden. Eden is the heart of creation. Its rivers feed the seas. Its breath feeds the skies. Its roots feed the earth with strength. Guard it, keep it, tend it, for this is your purpose."

Adam bowed low, and the garden answered him with its hum. He touched the grass, the bark, the stone, and each seemed to greet him. He bent to the rivers and saw his reflection, a face never before seen in creation. He pressed his hand to his chest, feeling the steady rhythm within, and whispered, "I am alive."

From the heights of heaven, the angelic forces looked on. Morning Star stood among them, radiant above all, brighter than flame. His gaze fixed upon the man of dust. He saw the Eternal draw near to Adam, speaking trust and purpose into him, a role denied even to angels.

And in the heart of the brightest, a shadow stirred.

Adam did not know this. His wonder was unbroken. He walked among the rivers, named the creatures, sang to the garden in his halting voice. But above him, unseen, Morning Star's song faltered. His eyes burned with envy, for the Eternal had given to a man of mud what even the brightest archangel could not hold.

Chapter Three

The Bone and the Breath

Adam walked in the garden and did as he was told. He touched the streams and named them. He looked upon the creatures and called them each by sound and meaning. He sang to the garden, halting but sincere, and the flowers opened wider when he passed.

Yet something stirred within him. In the stillness of night, when Eden grew quiet, he sat by the rivers and pressed his hand against the ground.

"Everything moves in pairs," Adam whispered. "Bird to bird, beast to beast, even rivers flow together into one. Why then am I alone?"

The Eternal's voice answered like a breath through the leaves.

"It is not good that you should be alone. From your side will come one who is flesh of your flesh and life of your life. You will walk together as the garden was meant to be kept."

Adam bowed his head. His eyes closed as the Eternal's breath moved over him, and a deep sleep fell upon him. The dust of his body stirred again, and from his side a bone was drawn. At the Eternal's word the bone was clothed with flesh, blood, and breath.

Adam woke and saw her.

Eve stood before him, her eyes wide, her breath catching as though the whole world had just poured into her lungs. Her hair glimmered with the light of Eden's rivers, her skin shone with purity untouched. She looked at Adam, and wonder softened her face.

"You are like me," she said, her voice trembling. "And yet not me."

Adam laughed, the sound breaking free like water over stone. He stepped closer, awe in every movement.

"You are bone of my bones," he whispered. "Flesh of my flesh. I will call you Woman, for you were drawn out of man."

Eve's lips curved with a smile. "And together?"

"Together we will walk the garden," Adam replied. His hand found hers, and Eden seemed to stir with new harmony, as though the very trees rejoiced.

From the heights, Morning Star watched. His radiance dimmed as his gaze fixed upon Eve. She was unlike anything of the heavens, unlike angels, unlike stars. She was fragile yet radiant, pure yet alive with promise. And she had been given to Adam, a creature of mud.

Morning Star's heart burned. He spoke softly to himself, words no other angel could hear.

"Why him and not me? Why should dust hold what starlight

cannot touch?"

Eve walked the garden with Adam, and their voices mingled like two streams joining. They touched the roots of the Trees, not in hunger, but in reverence, for the Eternal's warning still rang in Adam's heart: "The Tree of Life and the Tree of Knowledge are not for you. Their fruit carries power too great for flesh. Guard them, but do not eat."

Eve listened when Adam spoke those words, her head tilted in innocence. "If they are not for us, why do they stand here in the garden?"

Adam hesitated, his hand brushing against hers. "Because Eden is not only for us. It is the heart of all creation. From these Trees the world receives life and order. To eat from them is to take more than what we were given. And the Eternal said we will die if we touch them."

Eve lowered her eyes, thoughtful, yet still untroubled. She pressed her hand to Adam's chest, feeling the rhythm of his breath. "Then let us guard them. Together."

And Eden was filled with peace. Yet above them, Morning Star's envy grew like a fire that no song could extinguish.

Chapter Four

The Radiant Watcher

Morning Star entered Eden, his form clothed in brilliance. His radiance shimmered like fire upon gold, his voice like distant thunder softened into song. The garden stirred as he walked, for even the trees felt the weight of his presence.

Eve was by the river, watching the fish leap in the current, her laughter light and free. Adam was further among the fields, calling names to the creatures, so for a time she stood alone.

The air shifted, and she turned. Morning Star stood before her.

Eve's eyes widened. She had glimpsed the angelic host from afar, yet never so near. His form was taller than Adam's, his face brighter, his gaze piercing yet strangely tender.

"You are not Adam," Eve said softly, though her voice was steady.

Morning Star bowed slightly, the light of his countenance almost overwhelming. "I am Morning Star, first among those who were made before you. I have walked the heavens, sung as the stars were born, and stood near the Eternal when the seas were set in their places."

Eve tilted her head, studying him. "Then why do you walk here, in Eden?"

"Because Eden is the heart of all," Morning Star answered, his tone smooth as flowing water. "And because I have seen you."

Eve's breath caught. She lowered her eyes, innocence still upon her face, yet curiosity stirred. "Seen me?"

"Of all that has been formed, nothing shines as you do," Morning Star said. "The angels are clothed in starlight. Adam is made of dust. But you, your beauty is unlike either. You are the song the Eternal did not sing until now."

Eve's cheeks warmed though she did not understand why. She folded her arms across herself, suddenly aware of her bare form, though she had never thought of it before.

"You speak strangely," she whispered. "Adam says I am made for him. Bone of his bone. Flesh of his flesh."

Morning Star's smile was bright, but envy smoldered beneath it. "And yet, are you not more than his reflection? You are your own. Do you not wonder why the Eternal placed you here, in the shadow of the two Trees? Do you not wonder what lies within their fruit?"

Eve's eyes drifted to the center of the garden. The Trees towered high, their roots humming like heartbeats. Adam's words returned to her. The Eternal has forbidden them. To touch them is to die.

She shook her head. "Adam says we must not eat. The Eternal told him so."

Morning Star's gaze deepened. "Adam was told not to eat. But you, did the Eternal speak this to you? Or do you believe only what Adam has said?"

Eve blinked, uncertain, caught between innocence and a rising curiosity.

From the fields Adam's voice rang out, calling her name. Eve turned toward the sound. When she looked back, Morning Star had stepped into the shadows of the trees, his radiance fading into the leaves.

Eve stood very still, the river's song filling the silence. She pressed her hand to her chest, her heart racing in a way she could not explain.

CHAPTER FIVE

The Eternal's Charge

The evening light softened over Eden. Adam and Eve sat by the river, their hands twined, their eyes lifted to the Trees that stood at the garden's heart. Their shadows fell long across the grass, reaching toward the very roots that pulsed beneath the soil.

The sound of the Eternal's voice filled the air like the wind through every leaf. It was not thunder. It was not fire. It was presence.

"Adam. Eve. You are keepers of the garden. The rivers you drink from rise here. The breath you draw is fed from here. The strength that fills every beast and bird flows from here. The balance of creation rests in Eden, and to you I give its care."

Adam bowed his head. His voice was steady, but humble. "We will tend it, Eternal. We will walk where You have spoken, and we will guard what You have set in our hands."

Eve pressed closer to Adam, her eyes lifted toward the Eternal's unseen presence. "We will keep it safe. Together."

The Eternal's voice lingered like a calm fire. "From every tree you may eat. Their fruit is your provision, their branches your shade. But the Tree of Life and the Tree of Knowledge are not for you. Their fruit bears a current too great for flesh. In the day you take from them, death will follow. Guard them, for they are not given to man but to the order of creation itself."

Adam lowered his gaze. "I understand."

Eve looked upon the Trees, her brow furrowed. She whispered, "Why then are they here with us?"

The Eternal's reply was patient, yet weighty. "Because Eden is not only for you. It is the root of the earth. The Trees are the pillars through which all receives life and order. You are not tested by them. You are charged to honor what they hold. To consume their fruit is to break the harmony of all."

Eve pressed her face into Adam's shoulder, and her voice was quiet. "Then we will guard them, as You command."

And the voice of the Eternal was silent once more, but His presence lingered like breath upon the garden.

Unseen among the shadows, Morning Star stood at the edge of the Trees. His eyes blazed with envy. He had heard the words, had felt their weight, and bitterness coiled tighter within him.

"Not tested," he whispered. "Guardians, not sons. Dust made to keep what starlight is forbidden. They walk in the presence of the Eternal while I am left watching. His love is theirs, not mine."

He turned his gaze to Eve, still leaning into Adam, her eyes full of innocence and questions not yet answered. His voice softened, though no one heard.

"You will see, daughter of dust. You will see more than he tells you."

CHAPTER SIX

The Whisper Beneath the Leaves

The garden was quiet beneath the high sun. Adam walked among the fields, naming the beasts that grazed, his voice rolling in song as he worked. Eve lingered by the center of the garden. The Trees towered before her, their branches heavy, their roots pulsing deep beneath the soil like the steady beat of a heart.

She gazed at them with wonder, tracing their branches with her eyes. The fruit of the Tree of Knowledge glimmered as if kissed by light itself. She drew closer, not touching, only watching.

A voice stirred the air. "Why do you linger here, Eve?"

She turned. Morning Star stood among the shadows of the branches, his radiance softened so that she did not fall back in fear. His form gleamed like gold in the dappled light, his eyes holding both fire and sorrow.

"I do not know," Eve answered honestly. "I only wonder."

"Wonder is no sin," Morning Star said gently. He stepped closer, his presence warm and alluring. "It is the gift of life to seek what is beyond. Tell me, what does Adam say of this tree?"

Her gaze lowered. "He says we must not eat. The Eternal told him so. To touch its fruit is to die."

Morning Star's voice was soft, almost tender. "And did the Eternal speak this to you? Or was it to Adam alone?"

Eve hesitated. She pressed her hand to her chest. "It was Adam who told me. I trust him."

Morning Star's lips curved in a smile that held both charm and bitterness. "Trust is good, but should not your own eyes be opened? Should you not know for yourself what is truth? If the Eternal feared for you, why place such a tree in your path at all?"

Eve looked up, her innocence wavering with curiosity. "He said it is not for us. That the fruit is too great for flesh."

Morning Star circled the Tree, his fingers brushing the air near its branches but not the fruit itself. "Too great, or too powerful? There is more here than he tells you. This fruit does not bring death, Eve. It awakens. It is knowledge. To taste it is to see as the angels see, to understand as the Eternal understands."

Her eyes widened, and her breath quickened. "To be like the Eternal?"

Morning Star's voice deepened, burning with envy hidden beneath sweetness. "Yes. To know good and evil. To see the truth of all things. He would keep you from this because He fears what you may become. Does He not show more love to Adam than to me, the brightest of His host? Does He not hide from you what should be yours?"

Eve trembled, torn between obedience and desire for what she did not yet understand. Her eyes rose to the fruit. Its skin glowed in the light, as though it breathed with the power of the world itself.

Morning Star stepped closer, his gaze fixed upon her. His voice was a whisper that seemed to come from within her own thoughts.

"You are more than dust. More than Adam's shadow. Taste, and your eyes will be opened."

Her hand lifted, hesitant, shaking. She touched the fruit. The garden seemed to hold its breath.

And from the fields, Adam's voice called her name.

Eve froze. Morning Star's eyes burned with both longing and command. "Choose, Eve. Choose for yourself."

CHAPTER SEVEN

The Breaking of Harmony

Eve stood before the Tree, her hand trembling against the fruit. Morning Star's words lingered like fire in her mind. "You are more than dust. More than Adam's shadow. Taste, and your eyes will be opened."

Her breath came quickly. She lifted the fruit, its skin glowing like a captured flame. She pressed it to her lips and bit.

The current surged through her body. Her eyes widened as if a veil had been torn away. She saw herself, bare and unguarded, fragile yet luminous. She turned to Morning Star, and for a moment he seemed more beautiful than ever, his radiance overwhelming her senses. She felt awakened, alive in a way she had never known.

Adam's voice rang from the fields. He came running, his face open with trust. "Eve!"

She turned toward him, her hand still holding the fruit. Her voice was unsteady but eager. "Adam, taste. See what I have seen. There is more than we were told."

Adam looked at her, then at the fruit in her hand. His breath caught. He remembered the Eternal's words, the warning that rang like thunder in his chest. Yet he saw Eve's eyes, wide with new awareness, and his heart faltered.

He reached, took the fruit, and ate.

The surge struck him. His eyes opened, and shame flooded him. He saw his nakedness, his frailty. The garden no longer wrapped him in peace. The colors dimmed, the air grew heavy, the harmony of Eden trembled. He turned from Eve and covered himself with trembling hands.

The ground quaked. The rivers roared. The Trees themselves shuddered. The Eternal's voice broke through Eden like a storm.

"Adam. Eve. Where are you?"

They hid among the branches, pressing leaves to their bodies, their hearts pounding with dread. Adam called out, his voice shaking.

"I heard You in the garden, and I was afraid, because I am naked. I hid myself."

The Eternal's voice thundered with sorrow. "Who told you that you are naked? Have you eaten from the Tree which I commanded you not to eat?"

Adam's eyes filled with fear. He turned to Eve, and his words stumbled. "The woman You gave me, she gave me the fruit, and I ate."

Eve cried out, her voice breaking. "The watcher deceived me. He said it would awaken me, and I ate."

Morning Star stepped from the shadows, his radiance

blazing in defiance. His smile was proud, his eyes fierce. "Yes, Eternal. They are awake now. They see. They are more than dust, and You cannot keep them blind forever."

The garden shook as the Eternal's wrath burned. "Morning Star, son of the dawn. You were the highest among the host, clothed in beauty and splendor. Yet your heart was lifted with pride. You sought to twist My creation. You deceived the woman. For this, you are cast down. Upon your belly you shall crawl. Dust you shall eat all the days of your existence. You will be an enemy to the seed of the woman, and though you strike at their heel, her seed will crush your head."

Morning Star's radiance shattered. His form twisted, his beauty stripped away. He fell to the ground, writhing, his body contorting into the shape of a serpent. His cry was no longer song, but hiss.

The Eternal turned to Eve. His voice was heavy with sorrow. "You will bear children in pain. Your desire will turn to your husband, and he will rule over you."

To Adam He said, "Because you listened and ate, the ground is cursed because of you. By toil and sweat you will eat from it all your days. Thorns and thistles will rise against you, and you will return to the dust from which you came."

The garden wept. The rivers darkened. The peace of Eden was broken.

At the gate of the garden, the Eternal placed the cherubim, their swords of flame cutting through the air, guarding the way to the Tree of Life. Adam and Eve were driven out, clothed in garments of skin, the garden closed behind them.

And the world outside waited, wide and empty, no longer bound by Eden's harmony.

Chapter Eight

East of Eden

The flames of the cherubim burned behind them, and the song of the garden was no more. Adam and Eve made their dwelling in the wilderness, their hands blistered, their faces weary. The ground was harder now, the air colder. Yet even there, the Eternal's breath stirred life, and the soil yielded enough for them to survive.

Cain was their firstborn, strong and restless, his eyes sharp as flint. Abel followed, gentler, with a gaze that lingered on the skies and the flocks he tended.

As they grew, Adam sat with them by the fire and spoke of Eden. His voice carried both sorrow and longing. "There was a time," he told them, "when I walked freely among rivers that never dried and fields that never withered. I touched the trees, and the earth answered me in harmony. My task was to nurture the garden, to guard the heart of creation. But I failed. I let the voice of deceit turn my steps, and now you see the cost in your mother's tears, in the sweat of my brow."

Eve held her sons close. Her eyes shone in the firelight. "Do not repeat what we did. Guard your hearts, for the deceiver lingers still."

Cain listened, his brow furrowed. Abel leaned against his mother, silent but thoughtful.

Morning Star lingered at the edge of their dwelling, his body pressed low to the earth, his hiss carried by the wind. His form was now the serpent, but his voice still bore the remnants of his radiance, soft and enticing. He slithered into Cain's field where the boy labored over the soil, his hands raw from breaking the hardened ground.

"Why do you toil so?" the hiss whispered. "Why should you sweat and bleed for a God who turned His face from your father? Do you not see their suffering? Your mother's pain? Your father's shame? What has He done to repay them?"

Cain gritted his teeth, striking the earth with his hand. "I see it. I cannot bear it."

The hiss coiled tighter into his thoughts. "Then give back to Him what He demands. Offer Him the fruit of your labor. Perhaps He will forgive. Perhaps the curse will lift, and your parents will no longer struggle."

Cain's heart stirred with the thought. That night, he spoke to Abel while the fire crackled low. "Brother, what if we could give something to the Eternal? Not only our labor, but the best of what we have. Perhaps He would look upon us and see our parents' pain and heal it."

Abel's eyes brightened with hope. "Yes. Perhaps He would. You bring the harvest, and I will bring from the flock. Together we will offer it, and He will remember us."

Eve overheard them and felt a trembling in her chest. She looked to Adam, her voice hushed. "Do you think He will accept it?"

Adam's gaze was heavy with memory. "The Eternal knows the heart more than the gift. Let them bring what they will. Let us see what His voice will say."

And so Cain gathered the fruits of his field, and Abel chose the firstborn of his flock. The brothers prepared their offering with hands eager and uncertain, their hearts filled with longing. They did not see the serpent's eyes glinting from the stones, watching, waiting, whispering still.

CHAPTER NINE

The Divided Flame

The day came when Cain and Abel brought their offerings to the Eternal.

Cain worked from dawn, gathering the fruits of the soil with care. He chose what seemed best, arranging grain and ripened harvest into baskets. Sweat clung to his brow, but in his heart, there was hope. If the Eternal accepted his gift, perhaps the curse upon his parents would ease. Perhaps toil would no longer weigh so heavy.

Abel led a lamb from his flock, its wool white, its breath warm against his hands. He looked upon the creature with tenderness, for it was the firstborn, the finest he had. He carried it with reverence, as if each step was a prayer.

Adam and Eve stood apart, their faces shadowed by firelight. Adam's hand tightened over Eve's. "If He accepts them," Adam whispered, "perhaps He has not forgotten us."

The brothers laid their offerings upon the stones. Cain poured out his fruits, the colors bright in the sun. Abel placed his lamb upon the altar, lifting it with trembling but willing hands.

The air stilled. Then fire fell from heaven. It consumed Abel's lamb in a blaze, the smoke rising in fragrant offering. The Eternal's presence stirred the ground, His favor resting upon Abel.

But Cain's fruits remained untouched. No flame came. The colors dulled, their fragrance fading into dust.

Cain's chest heaved. His lips parted, yet no words came. His heart pounded with shame and confusion.

In the silence of the field, the serpent stirred. Morning Star's voice slipped from the shadows, not bitter but strangely calm.

"Cain, do not despair. I whispered this offering to you so that the Eternal might see your labor and restore your house. I thought perhaps there was mercy still. But if He has turned away, it is not because of your hands. The Eternal does not look as men look. He has His own secrets."

Cain sank to his knees, his eyes hot with tears. "Why then? What more can I give?"

Morning Star watched, and for a breath his tone was softened, humbled by Cain's grief. "Perhaps He asks for the heart, not only the fruit. Perhaps He seeks the blood of devotion, as Abel has given."

Cain lifted his head, but his eyes burned with something more than sorrow. He saw his brother bowing low, his face lit by the fire of acceptance. And in that sight, Morning Star's own wound reopened.

Memories surged. The Eternal had once clothed him in beauty, yet favored dust over starlight. He had stood glorious among the host, yet the man of mud was chosen. He remembered the moment he was cast down, cursed to crawl, stripped of splendor.

Bitterness coiled like smoke through his voice. "Look, Cain. Even now, Abel is lifted high while you are brought low. It is as it has always been. The Eternal favors another, and you are forgotten. Will you bow your head forever?"

Cain's hands clenched, his jaw set. He rose from the ground, his eyes fixed on Abel, not with brotherly love but with rising envy.

And Morning Star's hiss thickened the air, no longer soft, no longer humbled. "You can take what is yours. You need not wait for His favor. Make your own."

Chapter Ten

The Field of Blood

The days after the offering were restless. Cain worked his fields with furious hands, striking the soil as if it had betrayed him. Abel moved quietly among his flocks, his voice soft as he called them by name. Adam and Eve felt the silence between their sons, but they did not see the storm building beneath Cain's chest.

Morning Star lingered near the stones of Cain's field, his body low, his hiss curling like smoke. His voice was steady, patient. "Why should Abel's flock rise in favor while your fields are despised? Why must the Eternal love him more than you?"

Cain pressed his forehead to the ground, his breath ragged. "I gave what I had. Why is it never enough?"

The whisper deepened, heavier than before. "Because He will always choose another. As He chose Adam over me, so He now chooses Abel over you. The Eternal has no justice. Take what He withholds. Claim it for yourself."

Cain's fists clenched. He rose to his feet, his eyes burning. He called to Abel, his voice sharp in the morning air. "Brother, come. Walk with me into the field. There is something I wish to show you."

Abel followed, unsuspecting. His smile was gentle, his step unguarded. "What troubles you, Cain? The Eternal has not turned His face from you. He asks only that you turn your heart to Him. Will you not try again?"

Cain's jaw tightened. His brother's voice stung, not in anger but in its quiet kindness. He stopped among the rows of grain, his hands trembling.

"I have tried," Cain muttered. "I have given. But He does not see me."

Abel laid his hand upon Cain's shoulder, his eyes full of compassion. "He sees, brother. He waits for you to rise above your anger."

The words broke something inside Cain. His envy flared into fury, and Morning Star's hiss coiled with it like flame to oil.

"He sees you," Cain spat. "Only you. Always you."

Before Abel could answer, Cain struck. His hands seized his brother, and rage blinded him. Abel cried out once, his voice echoing through the field, then fell silent as blood soaked the soil.

The earth shuddered. The ground drank the blood, and its cry rose like thunder to the heavens.

Cain staggered back, his chest heaving. His hands shook as he looked upon his brother's lifeless form. The whisper of the serpent lingered, cold and hollow.

"It is done. You are no longer forgotten."

But Cain's heart was not filled with triumph. It was filled with dread. The blood of Abel clung to him, a weight he could not cast off.

From the dwelling, Adam and Eve lifted their heads, their spirits struck with grief though they had not yet seen. Eve's hand clutched her chest, and she wept as if her heart had already known.

And Morning Star slipped back into the shadows, his hiss low, his voice bitter. "As I fell, so too has man. The curse is not mine alone."

CHAPTER ELEVEN

The Voice of the Ground

The day of offering came again. Adam and Eve prepared their sons, their hearts still heavy but hopeful. Eve pressed Cain's hand as he gathered his grain. "Bring the best of what you have, my son. The Eternal sees."

Cain's eyes flickered. He said nothing, but carried his baskets to the altar. His shoulders were tense, his face shadowed.

Abel did not come.

Adam looked across the field. "Where is your brother? He is always among the first to arrive."

Cain shifted the weight of his baskets. "He will not come," he muttered.

The family laid their offerings on the stones. Cain's fruit spilled before the altar, but the air was still. No fire fell. No presence stirred.

Then the Eternal's voice broke the silence. It was not thunder. It was sorrow. "Cain. Where is your brother Abel?"

Cain's jaw tightened. His eyes stayed fixed upon the altar. "I do not know. Am I my brother's keeper?"

The voice of the Eternal rose, heavy as a storm. "The voice of your brother's blood cries out to Me from the ground. What have you done?"

Adam's breath caught. Eve's hands flew to her mouth as tears spilled down her face. The air seemed to press down upon them all, thick with grief.

Cain's hands trembled. His chest heaved with rage and dread. "You did not see me when I gave. You did not hear me when I cried out. You saw only Abel. So, I gave You blood, as You favored. Is this not what You asked?"

The Eternal's voice shook the earth. "Abel's blood is not an offering. It is a curse upon you. Now you are cursed from the ground, which has opened its mouth to receive your brother's blood. When you work the soil, it will no longer yield for you. A wanderer you shall be, restless upon the earth."

Cain fell to his knees, his voice desperate. "My punishment is too great. I will be hidden from Your face. Anyone who finds me will kill me."

The Eternal's voice softened, though it carried still the weight of judgment. "I will place a mark upon you. No hand that finds you shall slay you. Yet you will walk the earth alone, far from this place."

The air grew still. The fire upon the altar dimmed. Cain rose, his face pale, his eyes hollow. He turned from his parents and walked into the wilderness, the shadow of his mark upon him.

Adam sank to the ground. Eve collapsed against him, her sobs breaking through the silence. "My son," she cried. "My sons."

The soil beneath them was darkened with Abel's blood, and the ground itself seemed to mourn.

From the shadows, the serpent lingered, silent now. His eyes glinted with cold fire as he slipped away.

CHAPTER TWELVE

The Wanderer's City

Cain walked eastward, the ground hard beneath his feet, the mark of judgment heavy upon his soul. The fire of the altar was far behind him, and the cries of his parents no longer reached his ears. He was alone.

But not wholly.

The serpent lingered, crawling in the dust, its hiss curling through the silence. Morning Star's eyes glowed faintly with a broken fire. "I thought you would kill me," he whispered. "The Eternal said the seed of man would strike me down. I waited for your hand, but it never came."

Cain looked at him with hollow eyes. "I do not need to kill you. I understand you. Both of us cast out. Both of us cursed. Both of us marked, yet not destroyed."

The serpent coiled in the dust, and a sound like laughter slipped from its mouth. "Then we walk together."

Cain was not alone long. Some of his younger sisters followed him into exile, drawn by blood, loyalty, or defiance of Adam's sorrow. Cain took them as wives, and from their union children were born. From the wilderness they carved a beginning. Stones were stacked, fields were sown, tents became dwellings, and Cain raised a city. He named it after his firstborn son, Enoch, so that his name would endure.

Morning Star slithered at his side, whispering in the nights. "Build higher. Stretch your walls wide. Let the world see what you have made. If the Eternal will not favor you, then let men honor you."

The city grew, and with it the hearts of men swelled with pride. They raised altars, not to the Eternal, but to strength, to the work of their hands. Cain ruled, his shadow long across the valley, and Morning Star's whispers wove into every stone.

But far above, the Watchers looked down.

Two hundred angelic forces beheld the earth, their eyes fixed on Cain's city, their hearts stirred by longing and rebellion. They had been given the task to oversee, to guard, to watch. But watching soured into envy, for they remembered how Morning Star had been cast out and saw in Cain's defiance the reflection of their own desires.

They gathered upon a great mountain and swore an oath together. Semjaza, chief among them, lifted his voice. "Why should we remain as caretakers, bound in servitude to men of dust? Let us descend, and men will worship us as gods. We will rule, not serve."

Yet not all agreed. Azazel rose against him. "No. We will not rule them as tyrants. We will share with them what has been hidden. Let them live free of the Eternal's restraint. Let them know the secrets He feared we would carry."

Their voices divided. Some longed to be worshiped, clothed in power. Others longed to be adored, intoxicated by the beauty of women, the daughters of Adam and Eve, whose faces shone with the same wonder Eve once bore.

And so, they fell.

Two hundred descended into Cain's city. Some taught men to forge weapons, some to shape metal, some to read the stars and signs. Some whispered to women, taking them in their arms, birthing children not wholly human nor angelic. The harmony of earth broke beneath their feet.

And Cain's city swelled with wonders and with shadows, a place of power and confusion, a place the Eternal looked upon with grief.

CHAPTER THIRTEEN

The Rising Shadows

From the hills east of Eden, Adam watched the horizon. Smoke rose from Cain's city, pillars of fire against the sky. Strange sounds carried on the wind, the ringing of metal, the cries of voices raised in songs not sung to the Eternal.

Eve stood beside him, her face pale. "That is not the labor of the soil," she whispered. "That is something else."

Adam's voice was heavy. "Cain builds what I cannot. He has raised walls, forged tools, and his children multiply. Yet his works are not his alone. The whispers I once heard in the garden now speak in his streets."

For the Watchers had descended. Their presence was no longer hidden. They walked among men in forms that dazzled and terrified, teaching them arts unknown. Semjaza commanded worship. He raised altars in his name, demanding incense and sacrifice. The people bowed before him as before a god.

Azazel gave freely of knowledge. He showed men how to cut stone and shape weapons, how to polish metals and mark the heavens with signs. He gave women the secrets of adornment, the mixing of colors, the crafting of ornaments to set upon their faces. He told them, "You are not slaves. You are free. Take what the Eternal has kept from you."

And many of the Watchers, seeing the beauty of Adam's daughters, desired them. They took them as wives, and from their union came children of unnatural strength and stature. Giants walked the earth, fierce and proud, their voices shaking the ground.

Adam fell to his knees at the sight from afar. "The earth groans," he said, his face in his hands. "What I tended in Eden has been twisted. The fruit of my son's pride has become a snare for all."

Eve wept. "Did we not bring enough sorrow? Must our children bring more?"

The Eternal looked upon the earth, and His heart was pierced with grief. For men no longer called on His name, but on the names of angels. Temples rose to those who were never gods. Altars smoked with sacrifices not offered to Him. Blood was poured for the giants, and the harmony of creation trembled.

Morning Star slithered through Cain's streets, watching with bitter satisfaction. "See how they bow," he hissed. "Not to the Eternal, but to those who rebel. My curse was not wasted. My wound has become theirs."

And the heavens shook with sorrow, for rebellion had multiplied, and shadows spread across every valley.

CHAPTER FOURTEEN

The Cry of the Earth

From the wombs of Adam's daughters came children unlike any before them. Their limbs stretched long, their bodies towered, their voices thundered like drums. The giants walked among men, and wherever they stepped the ground trembled.

At first, they were admired. Cain's city sang songs of their strength. They raised stones that no man could lift, carved monuments that touched the sky, and broke the earth open to build halls of shadow. Men looked upon them and called them heroes.

But admiration turned to fear. The giants hungered beyond reason. Fields could not sustain them. Herds vanished, rivers thinned, and still they desired more. They seized what was not theirs, crushing men beneath their feet. They devoured not only the harvest of the ground but the flesh of animals and even of men.

Blood ran in the streets of Cain's city, and the earth drank deeply. Mothers hid their children. Fathers raised weapons in vain. The voices of men lifted not in songs but in screams.

The Watchers looked on with divided hearts. Semjaza reveled in it. "Now men will never rise against us," he declared. "They will cower, and their worship will remain ours."

Azazel turned his face away, though his teachings had already spread like fire. "This is not freedom," he muttered, yet his words were powerless against what had begun.

And Morning Star hissed with dark delight, circling at the feet of giants. "See what comes when creation is twisted. See how the Eternal's precious dust destroys itself."

From the hills, Adam and Eve heard the echoes of violence. They saw the fires at night, red against the sky. Eve wept, clutching her children close. Adam bowed his head, his voice breaking. "The ground that bore us now drinks our blood. Creation cries out against itself."

And the earth did cry. The fields torn by giants, the rivers drained by their thirst, the voices of men and women wailing for deliverance all rose upward like smoke.

The heavens trembled with the sound, and the throne of the Eternal was not silent. His heart was pierced with grief, and His patience thinned. For the harmony He had spoken into being now shook under the weight of corruption.

CHAPTER FIFTEEN

The Decree of Waters

The cries of the earth rose like smoke, and the heavens were heavy with sorrow. For every valley was filled with violence, every city with idols, every street with blood. The Eternal looked upon what had been shaped by His word, and His heart grieved.

And the Eternal spoke. "My spirit shall not dwell in man forever, for he is flesh and his days will be numbered. What was meant for harmony has become corruption. The breath I gave has turned against itself. The earth must be cleansed."

The Watchers stirred in fear, for they knew their rebellion had hastened this decree. The giants raged, stamping the ground as if they could defy the heavens themselves. But no cry, no monument, no altar of stone could silence the Eternal's judgment.

Morning Star hissed in the dust, his laughter thin and cold. "He will break them all, as He broke me. The Eternal cannot keep what He creates. He destroys what He loves." Yet even in his laughter there was unease, for the decree was final.

The Eternal spoke again. "I will send waters upon the earth, and they will cover the mountains. Every tower men have built will sink beneath the deep. Every altar raised to false gods will be washed away. The knowledge of the Watchers will be buried in silence. Even the monuments that scrape the skies will crumble, their power stripped. Only what I preserve shall remain."

And the heavens darkened. Clouds gathered, heavy and endless. The winds carried whispers of the storm to come. Men looked to the skies in fear, but their hearts still clung to idols. Giants roared, Watchers argued, and Cain's city swelled with confusion.

Yet in the line of Adam there remained a man of quiet heart, one who listened still for the voice of the Eternal. His name was Noah.

CHAPTER SIXTEEN

The Ark of Obedience

In the days when the giants consumed the earth and the Watchers walked among men, there was one who remained untouched by their corruption. His name was Noah, son of Lamech, of the line of Seth, the child who had replaced Abel.

While men built altars to false gods, Noah lifted his prayers to the Eternal. While Cain's city rang with iron and blood, Noah's dwelling was marked by quiet labor and reverence. He walked humbly, tending the soil without greed, offering what he had in thanksgiving, not demand.

The Eternal looked upon Noah and found favor in him. His heart was not lifted by pride nor swayed by whispers. He alone listened.

And the Eternal spoke to him in the stillness of night. "Noah, the end of all flesh has come before Me. The earth is filled with violence because of them. Behold, I will destroy them with the earth. But you, Noah, I will preserve. Build for yourself an ark of wood, with rooms within, and cover it inside and out with pitch. You and your sons, your wife, and your sons' wives shall enter it. With you I will preserve every living creature, two of each, to keep them alive upon the earth."

Noah bowed low, his face pressed to the ground. His heart trembled, yet he did not argue. He rose at dawn and told his family what the Eternal had spoken. His wife's eyes filled with tears, yet she nodded. His sons gathered tools, their wives gathered wood and tar, and together they began the labor.

As the ark rose plank by plank, the people mocked. "What is this madness?" they jeered. "A ship in the hills? Has the Eternal spoken to you, when He no longer speaks to men?" Giants roared with laughter, their voices shaking the valley. Watchers sneered from afar, whispering of futility.

But Noah's hands did not falter. Each blow of the hammer was a prayer, each plank a testimony. He did not build for men's approval, but for the Eternal's command.

Morning Star slithered near, watching with narrowed eyes. "So, He chooses again," he hissed. "Another favored son, while the rest are cast away. Will you endure, Noah, when the waters come? Or will you fall as all before you have fallen?"

Noah did not answer. His silence was his defiance. His obedience was his weapon.

And the ark rose, a vessel of wood and faith, standing against the storm that gathered.

Chapter Seventeen

The Breaking Deep

The ark stood finished upon the hills, its walls sealed with pitch, its chambers ready. The animals gathered in twos and sevens, led not by man's hand but by the Eternal's command. Birds wheeled in the sky and settled upon its beams. Beasts of the field walked the ramp with steady steps. Even serpents slithered into the shadows of its hold.

The people watched in astonishment, but their wonder turned quickly to scorn. "See the fool's ark," they laughed. "It is filled with beasts and crawling things. Will they sail the seas with birds and goats?" Giants roared with laughter, their voices shaking the ground. The Watchers stood upon the heights, sneering, their eyes filled with defiance.

But Noah and his family entered the ark, eight souls in all. His wife, his three sons, and their wives walked with him, their faces solemn, their hearts trembling yet steadfast. When the last of the creatures had entered, the Eternal Himself shut the door.

The sky darkened.

A silence fell, heavy as stone. Then thunder cracked across the heavens, and lightning split the sky. The fountains of the deep broke open, and waters surged from beneath the earth. The heavens poured torrents unceasing. Rivers rose, fields drowned, and valleys vanished.

The people ran to high ground, crying out for deliverance. They struck the ark with their fists, pleading for entrance, but the door remained shut. The giants raged, their voices drowned by the roar of waters. The Watchers fled, yet found no refuge.

Cain's city was swallowed. Towers sank into the depths, monuments of stone toppled, and altars to false gods dissolved in the flood. The works of the Watchers were broken, their secrets washed away, their power silenced.

Morning Star lifted his head above the rushing flood, hissing through the storm. "So He destroys again. He wipes away all memory, all glory. The Eternal builds only to unmake." Yet his words were choked by the waters that rose higher, and even he was swallowed into silence.

Inside the ark, the cries of the dying beat against the walls like the sea itself. Noah pressed his face into the wood, his tears mingling with the rain. "Eternal," he whispered, "Your will is done."

And the waters covered the face of the earth. Mountains vanished. Valleys drowned. The world was undone, and only silence remained above the endless deep.

CHAPTER EIGHTEEN

The Endless Waters

The rains did not cease. For forty days the heavens poured without rest, and the fountains of the deep gave forth their flood. The earth disappeared beneath the endless sea. Mountains were swallowed. Valleys were buried. Cities and altars and monuments were gone as if they had never been.

The ark rose upon the waters, lifted from the ground. It drifted in the vast expanse, a single vessel in an ocean without shore. Inside, Noah and his family prayed, their voices trembling with awe and fear. Around them the beasts were silent, subdued by the hand of the Eternal.

Day after day the waters rose higher until no peak remained. All flesh outside the ark perished. The laughter of giants, the boasts of kings, the whispers of the Watchers, every sound was silenced. Only the roar of waters remained, a hymn of judgment.

Noah pressed his hand against the wooden wall, his voice low. "The Eternal has unmade the earth. Yet if He has preserved us, then He has not forgotten His covenant."

Time passed, slow and heavy. The rains ceased, but the waters still covered the face of the world. The ark drifted under a sky emptied of stars. Silence stretched across the deep, broken only by the creak of wood and the cry of a bird within.

At last, the Eternal remembered Noah. The winds stirred, sweeping across the waters. The floods began to withdraw. The fountains of the deep were sealed, the torrents from heaven restrained. Slowly the waters fell, revealing once more the shoulders of mountains.

The ark came to rest upon the heights of Ararat, its hull wedged in stone. Noah opened the window and released a raven. It flew across the expanse, but finding no place to land, it returned. Later he sent a dove, and in its beak, it carried an olive leaf, green and living.

Noah wept as he held the leaf. "Life remains," he whispered. "The Eternal will begin again."

And so, the ark waited, surrounded by silence, upon a world reborn through ruin.

Chapter Nineteen

The Covenant of Renewal

When the ground was dry, the Eternal spoke to Noah. "Come out of the ark, you and your wife, your sons and their wives. Bring out every living creature with you, that they may swarm upon the earth, be fruitful, and multiply again."

Noah obeyed. He opened the great door, and light poured into the ark. His family stepped out, their feet sinking into fresh soil, the scent of earth rising after long silence. The beasts poured forth in streams, birds lifting into the sky, herds scattering into valleys, and creeping things rushing across the ground. Life began to move again upon the world.

Noah looked across the empty land and fell to his knees. He gathered stones and built an altar to the Eternal. Upon it he laid clean offerings, the first of the new earth's harvest. The smoke rose into the heavens, and the Eternal smelled the offering with satisfaction.

The Eternal spoke within Himself. "Never again will I curse the ground because of man, though his heart is inclined to evil from youth. Never again will I strike down all living things as I have done. While the earth remains, seedtime and harvest, cold and heat, summer and winter, day and night shall not cease."

And the Eternal blessed Noah and his sons. "Be fruitful and multiply. Fill the earth and rule over it. Every beast of the field, every bird of the sky, every creature that moves will fear you. Into your hands they are delivered. But the blood of life is Mine. Whoever sheds the blood of man, by man shall his blood be shed, for in My image man was made."

Then the Eternal set a bow in the clouds, a great arc of color stretched across the sky. The light shimmered above the earth, bright against the storm's fading shadow. "This is the sign of the covenant that I make between Me and you and every living creature. Never again shall the waters become a flood to destroy all flesh. When the bow appears in the clouds, I will remember My covenant with you."

Noah lifted his eyes to the bow, his face wet with tears. His family stood with him, silent and reverent. The beasts moved across the fields, the sky cleared, and the world seemed new again.

And so, the ark was left behind, resting in the mountains, a monument to survival and obedience. The earth breathed once more, cleansed by waters, bound by promise.

Chapter Twenty

The Tower and the Scatter

The sons of Noah multiplied, filling the valleys and plains. Their children spread into tribes, and soon the fields were alive with voices. But they were not of one mind.

"Let us stay together," said Nimrod, a son of Cush. His voice carried over the people. "If we scatter, we will be forgotten. Let us make a city, and in its heart a tower that rises to the heavens. Its top will reach the skies, and no man will wander again."

The people murmured in agreement. Women gathered clay, men baked bricks, children carried stones. Fires burned night and day as the tower's base rose higher.

Some among them hesitated. "Is it not enough that the Eternal saved us?" one of Noah's younger grandsons asked. "Should we not spread as He commanded?"

But Nimrod's eyes flashed. "He gave us the earth. If He scattered our fathers with waters, we will bind ourselves with stone. If He cursed Cain to wander, we will build where no curse can reach us. Let us rise where even the Eternal cannot bring us down."

The restless spirits of the giants circled unseen, whispering to the builders. "Raise it higher. Shape it in our honor. Build altars to the stars." The hands of men obeyed, and songs to false gods rose with the tower's height.

Noah, now old, came with his sons to the edge of the city. He saw the work and shook his head. "This is pride, not remembrance," he said. "Did we not live through the waters? Did the bow in the heavens mean nothing?"

But the people only laughed. "Your days are behind you, old man. We will not live in fear of another flood. We will master the heavens."

The Eternal sent an angel to walk among them. Clothed in brightness, his presence unsettled the workers. He moved through their midst, listening to their speech, watching their hearts. Then he lifted his face to the skies.

"They are one people," he said. "With one tongue they plot rebellion, and nothing will restrain their pride. It is time."

At once the voices of the workers broke into confusion. A man called for a brick, but his brother answered with words he could not understand. A woman passed water to her child, but her neighbor shouted at her in a strange tongue. Anger flared, fear rose, and the city turned to chaos.

"Why do you speak like a stranger?" one man cried. "Have you cursed me?"

"No," another shouted back, "it is you who mock me!"

They dropped their tools, their unity shattered. Families clung together, but tribes turned from one another. Soon they left the tower behind, scattering into valleys, forests, mountains, and coasts, each carrying their own tongue.

Nimrod stood at the base of the unfinished tower, his fists clenched. "The Eternal has divided us. He has stolen our strength. But I will not forget. One day, man will rise again."

The angel lifted his gaze heavenward. The tower loomed unfinished, a monument to pride undone. The people spread across the earth, their voices many, their gods multiplied.

And the restless spirits followed them, whispering into every land.

Chapter Twenty-One

The Shadows Over the Nations

The people left Shinar in confusion, each tribe speaking a tongue the others could not understand. Families clung together, yet neighbors turned into strangers. They carried memories of the tower, but with every mile the lesson faded. Pride was not broken, only divided.

A man stood by the river with his kin. "The Eternal has cursed our speech," he said bitterly. "We will raise stones to other powers who do not scatter us."

His wife placed carved wood in the water. "This will be our god. It will hear us when the Eternal will not."

In the mountains, another tribe lifted their hands to the sun. "It warms us, it feeds our fields. Surely it is greater than the unseen voice of Noah's God."

By the sea, a chieftain poured wine into the waves. "The waters cover the earth. They are the strongest of all. Let us honor them with blood and song."

And the restless spirits of the giants followed. They whispered in every land. "Raise stones to us. Carve our likeness. Burn incense and offer flesh, and we will grant you victory, pleasure, and strength."

Men listened. Women bowed. Kings commanded altars to be built in their names. Children were sacrificed in flames, blood spilled upon mountains, incense smoked in valleys. Idols filled the cities, each with eyes that could not see and mouths that could not speak, yet behind them the spirits laughed, feeding on the devotion of men.

From afar, Noah's sons of Shem's line remembered. They gathered their families around the fire and spoke of the covenant, of the rainbow that still crowned the sky after the rains. "The Eternal has not forgotten us," they whispered to their children. "One day He will raise a seed to crush the deceiver and restore His promise."

But across most of the earth, darkness spread. Nations fought for the favor of false gods. Kings lifted their swords in their names. Queens burned incense to shadows. The spirits moved unseen, stirring wars, vanity, and fury.

The heavens looked down in sorrow, waiting for the Eternal's voice to speak again.

EPILOGUE

The Echo Still Heard

In the beginning, man's purpose was simple. Adam was placed in Eden to nurture it, to guard its rivers and its trees, to care for the life that sprang from the Eternal's word. He was not made to build towers or kingdoms, but to walk in harmony with the garden and the Creator.

Yet that purpose was broken. The serpent whispered, the Watchers descended, the giants consumed, and the course of mankind was twisted. The world filled with altars to shadows, monuments to pride, and wars born of envy. What was given as a trust became a contest. What was meant to be peace became complication.

Through every age the spirits of rebellion have deceived, bending man's heart away from its first calling. And now, even in the present, it is hard to tell what worship rises to the Eternal and what devotion is swallowed by shadows. We build for ourselves. We chase power and call it progress. We raise towers of stone, steel, and glass, forgetting the simple task first entrusted to Adam: to tend, to guard, to keep.

This book may stir controversy, for it does not tell a tale of comfort. It is not meant to open eyes in arrogance, but to remind in humility. It is not for us to decide the measure of our greatness or the weight of our destiny. The Eternal alone holds that power. His presence is fire beyond fire, His energy bursting beyond what heaven or earth can contain. To draw too close would undo us in an instant.

So live. Live as Adam once lived, before the fall. Take care of what has been given today. Guard the earth, its waters, its air, its creatures. Seek not to conquer, but to preserve. For no sacrifice of blood or stone can cleanse what is broken. Only we, with the knowledge of our ancestors' mistakes, can choose to live differently.

Let us look back to our roots. The Tree of Life. The Tree of Knowledge. The gift of creation itself. Let us take care, for in this care lies the echo of Eden, and in that echo, we may yet remember the purpose we have forgotten.

END

Author's Note

When I began writing *Echoes of Eden*, I did not set out to rewrite scripture. I set out to imagine the story beneath the story, the whispers between the lines, the shadows that might have shaped the world we inherited.

From Adam's first purpose in Eden, to nurture and care for creation, our history has grown more complicated. The Watchers, the giants, the scattered nations, and the restless spirits are not only echoes of the past. They are reflections of what we still face today. Pride, envy, lust for power, the twisting of what was meant for harmony, these remain part of our world.

This book may stir questions, perhaps even controversy. It is not written to replace faith, but to spark reflection. It is not to dictate what we must believe, but to remind us that the Eternal remains beyond our grasp, bursting with energy no earthly or heavenly being can contain. Our place is not to wield His power, but to live within the purpose first entrusted to Adam: to tend, to nurture, and to guard what has been given.

If we look back to the roots, the Tree of Life and the Tree of Knowledge, we remember where we came from. And perhaps, if we choose wisely, we can also remember what it means to live.

Thank you for walking this journey with me. May these echoes inspire you to see our world not with fear, but with care.